JENNY'S BIRTHDAY BOOK

MORE BOOKS ABOUT JENNY BY ESTHER AVERILL

Jenny and the Cat Club: A Collection of Favorite Stories about Jenny Linsky

Jenny Goes to Sea

Jenny's Moonlight Adventure

Hotel Cat

JENNY'S BIRTHDAY BOOK

by Esther Averill

THE NEW YORK REVIEW CHILDREN'S COLLECTION
New York

THIS IS A NEW YORK REVIEW BOOK
PUBLISHED BY THE NEW YORK REVIEW OF BOOKS

Copyright © 1954 by Esther Averill
All rights reserved.

Published in the United States of America by
The New York Review of Books
435 Hudson Street
New York, NY 10014
www.nyrb.com

Library of Congress Cataloging-in-Publication Data

Averill, Esther Holden.
Jenny's birthday book / by Esther Averill.
p. cm. — (New York Review children's collection)
Summary: With her brothers and her friends, the little black cat named Jenny celebrates her birthday in the park.
ISBN 1-59017-154-3 (alk. paper)
[1. Cats—Fiction. 2. Birthdays—Fiction. 3. New York (N.Y.)—History—20th century—Fiction.] I. Title. II. Series.
PZ7.A935Jeb 2005
[E]—dc22
2004029977

ISBN 978-1-59017-154-7

Cover design by Louise Fili Ltd.

This book is printed on acid-free paper.
Manufactured in China
5 7 9 10 8 6 4

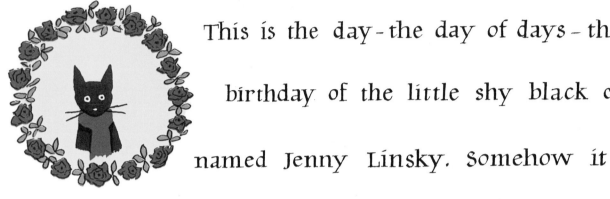 This is the day - the day of days - the
birthday of the little shy black cat
named Jenny Linsky. Somehow it
seems as if the sun were shining and the roses
blooming just for her. Outside Jenny's window stand
her brothers, Checkers and Edward, ready to take
her to a birthday picnic in the park.

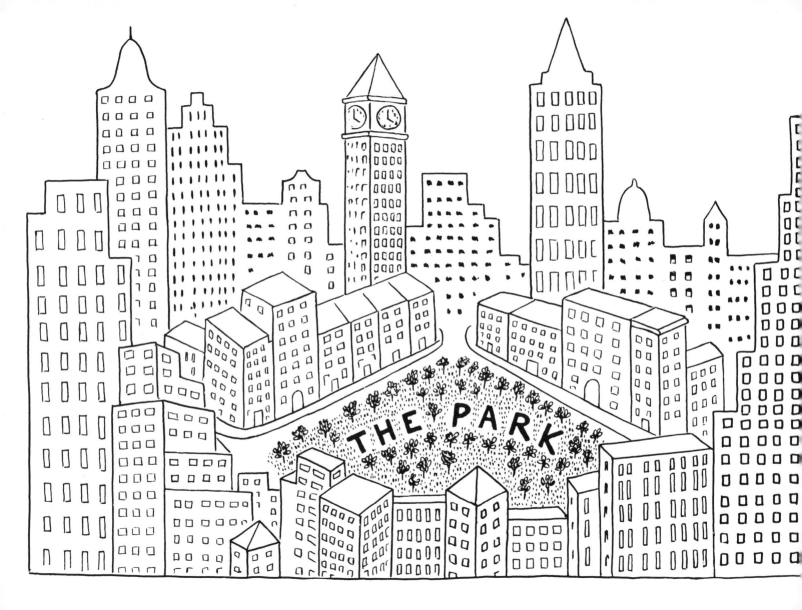

The park lies in a busy part

of New York City.

As Jenny and her brothers scamper

through the streets, they watch

carefully for the traffic light— the

green light that means Go!

They pass the flower shop.

Then, at the fish shop, Jenny meets the twins, Romulus and Remus, carrying a birthday present.

"Don't open it until we reach the park," they say.

The next stop is

the fire house

where...

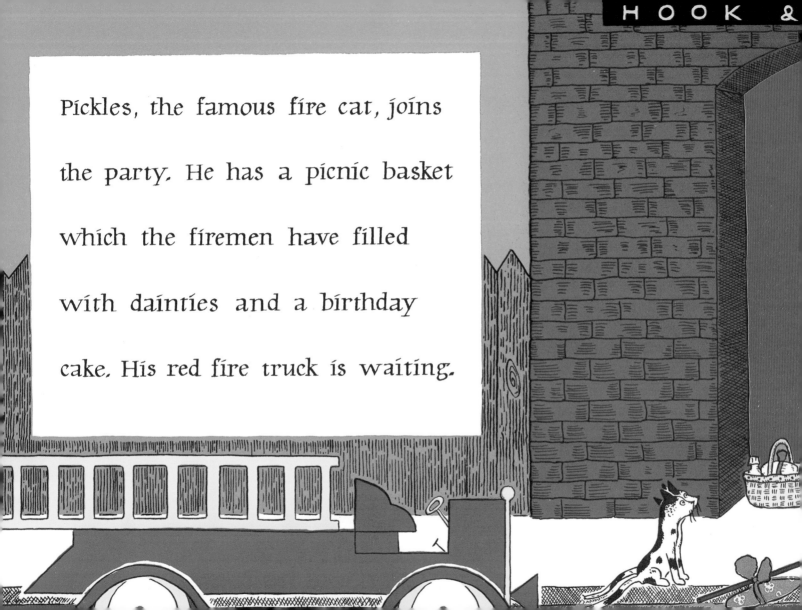

Pickles, the famous fire cat, joins the party. He has a picnic basket which the firemen have filled with dainties and a birthday cake. His red fire truck is waiting.

HOOK &

Pickles starts the engine of his fire truck.

"All aboard for Jenny's birthday picnic in the park!" he cries.

"We mustn't forget Florio," Jenny reminds him as she climbs onto the truck.

While the truck speeds up the avenue towards Florio's house, Pickles sounds his siren.

They pick up Jenny's old

friend, Florio, who wears

an Indian feather in honor

of the birthday.

Then the truck heads for

the flowery park.

Other cats have heard the siren of the fire truck. These cats, too, are loyal friends of Jenny Linsky. So they follow the trail of the truck and reach the park just as the picnic supper is being spread out on the cool, green grass.

Friends, young and old, troop into the park, singing:

Greetings we bring

And merrily sing

Happy birthday to you!

May dear little Jenny

Have many and many

More birthdays come true.

There is food for all the cats who come a-running.

The twins have given Jenny a delicious bluefish.

The big moon rises while

the feast is being eaten.

After the feast, Jenny's friends gather around her.

"Jenny," they say, "a birthday cat may do whatever she likes best. Please name your wish."

"I'd love to dance," she answers shyly.

"Please name the dance," they beg.

And Jenny cries excitedly, "The sailor's hornpipe!"

They dance the sailor's hornpipe in the moonlit park.

The two big fighters, Sinbad and
The Duke, dance gently with a
little stranger who has wandered
into Jenny's party.

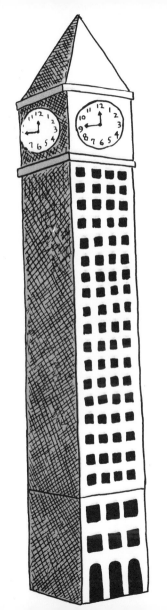

When it grows late, it's time for bed.

The friends pile into Pickles' fire truck,

and he drives the little black cat

to her home.

She thanks them one and all for giving

her a happy birthday. Then...

Jenny waves

good night.

Sleepily she

climbs the

stairs to go

to bed.

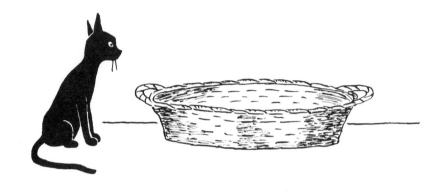

Before she lies down in her basket, Jenny makes a

little prayer: "Please may all cats everywhere have

happy birthdays when their birthdays come."

Soon she is sleeping-

dreaming of her

birthday picnic.

The
End

ESTHER AVERILL (1902–1992) began her career as a storyteller drawing cartoons for her local newspaper. After graduating from Vassar College in 1923, she moved first to New York City and then to Paris, where she founded her own publishing company. The Domino Press introduced American readers to artists from all over the world, including Feodor Rojankovsky, who later won a Caldecott Award.

In 1941, Averill returned to the United States and found a job in the New York Public Library while continuing her work as a publisher. She wrote her first book about the red-scarfed, mild-mannered cat Jenny Linsky in 1944, modeling its heroine on her own shy cat. Averill would eventually write twelve more tales about Miss Linsky and her friends (including the I Can Read Book *The Fire Cat*), each of which was eagerly awaited by children all over the United States (and their parents, too).

TITLES IN THE NEW YORK REVIEW
CHILDREN'S COLLECTION

ESTHER AVERILL
Jenny and the Cat Club

ESTHER AVERILL
Jenny Goes to Sea

ESTHER AVERILL
Jenny's Birthday Book

DINO BUZZATI
The Bears' Famous Invasion of Sicily

EILÍS DILLON
The Island of Horses

ELEANOR FARJEON
The Little Bookroom

RUMER GODDEN
An Episode of Sparrows

NORMAN LINDSAY
The Magic Pudding

ERIC LINKLATER
The Wind on the Moon

BARBARA SLEIGH
Carbonel: The King of the Cats

T. H. WHITE
Mistress Masham's Repose

REINER ZIMNIK
The Crane